BOUNTY HUNTER 2125

A TIME TRAVEL ADVENTURE

VICTORIA RUSH

VOLUME 5

RILEY'S TIME TRAVEL ADVENTURES - BOOK 5

COPYRIGHT

ALSO BY VICTORIA RUSH

Adult Fairytales:

The Enchanted Forest: An Erotic Fairytale

The Land of Giants: An Erotic Fairytale

The Dragon's Lair: An Erotic Fairytale

Witch's Brew: An Erotic Fairytale

The Mage's Spell: An Erotic Fairytale

The Mermaid Lagoon: An Erotic Fairytale

The Coven: An Erotic Fairytale

Rapunzel: An Erotic Fairytale

The Seven Dwarfs: An Erotic Fairytale

The Land of Mutants: An Erotic Fairytale

The Erotic Temple: A Sexy Fairytale (Coming Soon)

Erotica Themed Bundles:

Voyeur: Lesbian Erotica Bundle

Public Affairs: A Lesbian Anthology

Futa Fantasies: The Ladyboy Collection

Threesomes: The Lesbian Collection

Threesomes - Volume 2: The Lesbian Collection

First Time: A Lesbian Anthology

Hedonism: An Erotic Anthology

Switch Hitters: Bisexual Erotica

Taboo Erotica: The Lesbian Series

BDSM: The Lesbian Collection

Party Games: The Erotic Collection

Party Games 2: The Erotic Collection

All Girl 1: Lesbian Erotica Bundle

All Girl 2: Lesbian Erotica Bundle

All Girl 3: Lesbian Erotica Bundle

All Girl 4: Lesbian Erotica Bundle

Erotic Fairytale Bundles:

Clover's Fantasy Adventures: Books 1 - 5

Clover's Fantasy Adventures: Books 6 - 10

Erotic Fantasy:

Pirate's Bounty: A Time Travel Adventure

Wild West: A Time Travel Adventure

Private Riley: A Time Travel Adventure

Cleopatra's Secret: A Time Travel Adventure

Bounty Hunter 2125: A Time Travel Adventure

Ninja Assassin: A Time Travel Adventure

The 300: A Time Travel Adventure

Arabian Nights: An Erotic Fairytale (coming soon...)

Steamy Time Travel Bundles:

Riley's Time Travel Adventures: Books 1 - 5

Lesbian Erotica:

The Dinner Party: Lesbian Voyeur Erotica

The Darkroom: Bisexual Voyeur Erotica

Naked Yoga: Lesbian Transgender Erotica

Nude Cruise: Bisexual Voyeur Erotica

Rush Hour: Taboo Public Sex

The Girl Next Door: First Time Lesbian Erotic Romance

Girls' Camp: Lesbian Group Sex

Wet Dream: Ladyboy Fantasy Erotica

The Convent: Taboo Sex with a Nun

Sex Robot: A Dream Sex Machine

The Personal Trainer: Getting Pumped at the Gym

The Dominatrix: BDSM Lesbian Domination

Webcam Chat: Lesbian Online Sex

Paint Me: A Kinky Bodypainting Workshop

The Toy Party: Girls Sharing Sex Toys

The Costume Party: Strapping One On

Swedish Sauna: Lesbian Group Sex

The Therapist: Taboo Lesbian Erotica

Elevator Shaft: Bisexual Threesomes Erotica

Ladyboy: Lesbian Transgender Erotica

Peep Show: Lesbian Voyeur Erotica

The Dare: Public Sex Erotica

Maid Service: Lesbian Threesomes Erotica

The Hitchhiker: First Time Lesbian Erotica

The Housesitter: Spycam Lesbian Erotica

The Spa: Lesbian Group Orgy

Parlor Games: Blindfold Sex Party

The Exchange Student: First Time Lesbian Erotica

The Hostel: Bisexual Group Erotica

The Harem: Lesbian Erotic Romance

The Orient Express: Lesbian Voyeur Erotica

The First Lady: A Forbidden Lesbian Erotic Romance

The Slave: Lesbian BDSM Erotica

The Masseuse: Lesbian Sensuous Erotica

Too Close for Comfort: Lesbian Forbidden Erotica

Naked Twister: A Wild Party Game

Lexi: The Sex App (Lesbian Fantasy Erotica)

Call Girl: Lesbian Bisexual Threesomes Erotica

Circle Jill: Lesbian Masturbation Workshop

The Viewing Room: Masturbation Voyeur Erotica

Spin the Bottle: A Kinky Party Game

The Hair Salon: Lesbian Voyeur Erotica

Tribadism 1: Girls Only Sex Workshop

Tribadism 2: The Art of Scissoring

Tribadism 3: Threeway Hookups

The Kiss: A Game of Oral Sex

Pledge Week: Sorority Sisters

Carny Games 1: A Wild Sex Party

Carny Games 2: A Kinky Sex Party

Carny Games 3: An Erotic Sex Party

Dreamscape: An Artificial Reality Game

Glory Hole: Guess Who's On the Other Side

Joy Ride: A Late Night Erotic Bus Trip

The Blind Girl: An Erotic Romance(Coming Soon)

Lesbian Erotica Bundles:

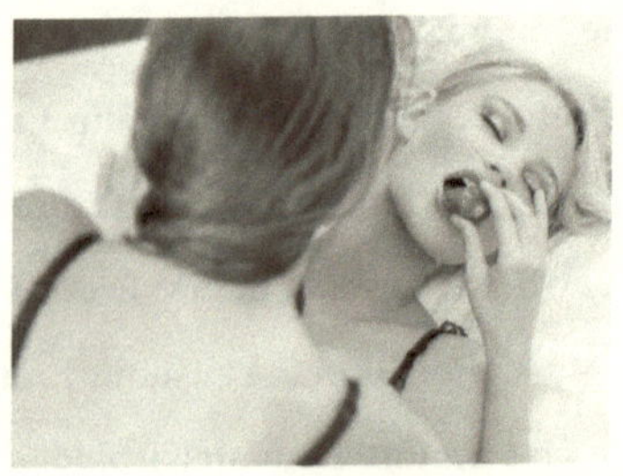

Jade's Erotic Adventures: Books 1 - 5

Jade's Erotic Adventures: Books 6 - 10

Jade's Erotic Adventures: Books 11 - 15

Jade's Erotic Adventures: Books 16 - 20

Jade's Erotic Adventures: Books 21 - 25

Jade's Erotic Adventures: Books 26 - 30

Jade's Erotic Adventures: Books 31 - 35

Jade's Erotic Adventures: Books 36 - 40

Jade's Erotic Adventures: Books 41 - 45

Jade's Erotic Adventures: Books 46 - 50

Fifty Shades of Jade: Superbundle

Standalone Stories:

The Polynesian Girl: A Lesbian EroticRomance

For the uninhibited...

WANT TO AMP UP YOUR SEX LIFE?

Sign up for my newsletter to receive more free books and other steamy stuff. Discover a hundred different ways to wet your whistle!

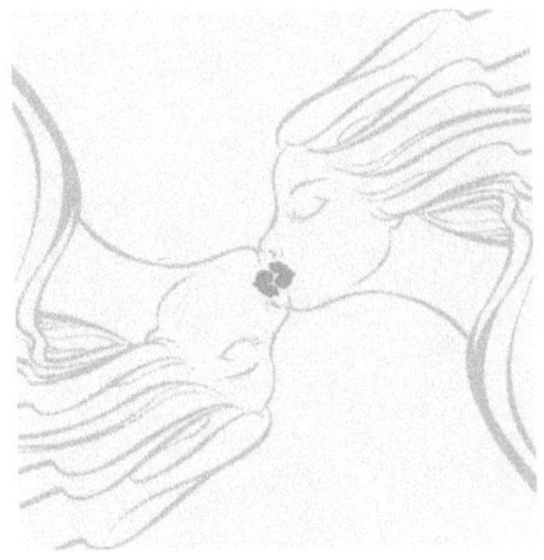

Victoria Rush Erotica

1

———

After her last adventure in ancient Egypt, Riley felt herself tumbling through the time machine portal once again, unsure where she'd land. A few minutes later, she felt her body thump down into the saddle of a motorcycle careening from side to side while chasing another speeding vehicle through a futuristic cityscape.

"Where the hell am I *now*?" she muttered to herself, suddenly realizing she was dressed in a head-to-toe, tight-fitting leather bodysuit, wearing a futuristic helmet with a heads-up display.

Then she glanced down, noticing her motorcycle didn't have any wheels and that she was riding on a cushion of air, jetting through space on some kind of rocket-propelled jet-ski.

"Well at least I'm appropriately *dressed* for the occasion this time," she smiled, tilting her body while she darted after the levitating motorcycle in front of her.

She focused her eyes on the heads-up display on her helmet visor, scanning the blinking message inches away from her face.

'Apprehend target with extreme caution,' the message read. 'Fugitive is armed. Bounty doubled if captured alive.'

Bounty? Riley thought, squinting her eyes. *Fugitive? Why am I chasing this person? And where is this place?*

She glanced ahead just in time to dodge a large truck passing through an elevated intersection, locking her electronic homing signal back on the motorcycle swerving wildly between the futuristic buildings.

This doesn't look like any place on earth. At least not anything from my time. Either the time machine pushed me forward in time, or this is some unfamiliar planet. Maybe both.

But right now, Riley had more pressing concerns than figuring out where she was and when. As her target swerved around the other levitating vehicles on the invisible road, it took all her strength and wits to maintain control of her rocket-propelled vehicle. It had the same feel and controls of a motorcycle, but without any surface contact on the road surface, it felt unnerving steering the vehicle through thin air. She glanced under her feet, noticing small ailerons tilting up and down on thin foils jutting out from the underside of the space cycle.

So they finally did it, she said to herself. *They finally invented a flying car. I don't know what powers this thing, but it's sure a damn sight faster than my old Triumph.*

As she gunned the throttle on the swept-back handlebars, she tilted her body, letting the wings of the craft guide her through the ethereal landscape while chasing the unknown bandit.

Whoever this guy is, he sure doesn't want to be caught, she thought, as slower-moving vehicles on the gossamer highway flashed their lights when the two vehicles jetted past them. *I'm not sure how much gravity exists is in this place, but I'm pretty sure if we crash into one of those weird buildings we're zipping past that I'll feel the effects of rapid deceleration just the same.*

Suddenly, a large helicopter flashing blue lights appeared directly in front of them, angling its nose down toward the illuminated thoroughfare. The bandit's brake lights lit up, and he tilted his bike on its side, trying to slide underneath it. As he spiraled out of control down the highway, Riley had to pitch hard to the right to avoid hitting the dipping skids of the chopper. When she saw the target lying on the road separated from his vehicle, she braked quickly, jumping off her motorcycle onto the invisible surface.

"Halt!" she yelled, unsure what the protocol was for apprehending the unknown perpetrator. "Face down with your hands over your head!"

The target took one look at Riley and the helicopter slowly swinging around to face them, then he pulled a strange-looking pistol from behind his back, firing a light stream in her direction. She ducked as the pulse jetted inches away from her head, then she reached down to her side, retracting the pistol from a holster on her side, firing it toward the assailant's torso.

Fuck it, she thought. *I don't care if they want this guy dead or alive. Right now, I just need to stop him from shooting me.*

The laser beam caught the man in the left shoulder and he reached up, screaming in pain.

"You *shot* me!" he said, dropping his pistol as he collapsed onto his knees.

"You tried to shoot me first," Riley said, walking slowly toward the man while holding her pistol steadily with two hands.

Her gun was unlike anything she'd handled before, much lighter and more powerful than the six-shooter she'd practiced firing on Madame's ranch in 1880's Wyoming.

Thank God for Ben's steady hand, she thought to herself, remembering the sexy cowboy who'd taught her how to shoot. *I guess a gun is a gun, no matter how advanced its technology. At least I still remember how to aim properly.*

While the outlaw winced in pain holding his bleeding shoulder, the helicopter landed slowly behind her, buffeting her body with the force of its powerful rotors.

"Good work, Vega," a man wearing a high-tech police uniform said, walking toward the perp with his firearm raised while two other officers followed closely behind. "We'll take it from here."

Vega? Riley said, shaking her head. *How do they know my name? And what am I supposed to do now?*

She watched the two junior officers grab the man and drag him toward the helicopter while the one who complimented her kept his pistol trained on his back.

"So what happens now?" Riley said as he passed by, barely giving her a sideways glance.

"You know the drill," he said. "You'll have to come back to the station to collect your prize. Though I don't know how happy the chief will be when he sees how banged up the skip is. You might have a few credits shaved off the top for bringing in damaged goods."

Riley peered at the trio trudging back to the chopper, then at the long line of backed up traffic waiting for the whirlybird to clear the lane.

"Do you mind if I follow you back there?" she said, unsure where the police station was.

"Suit yourself," the lead cop said. "Just don't stray too far behind. We'll be going off marked lanes and you don't want to get slammed by any crossing traffic."

As the helicopter took off into the air, Riley peered up,

noticing a latticework of crisscrossing aerial highways carrying a fast-moving stream of levitating space vehicles.

Man, those guys at Hanna-Barbera weren't far off, she said to herself as she climbed back onto her rocket bike. *This place looks just like Orbit City from the old animated TV series, The Jetsons.*

2

After Riley followed the police helicopter back to the police station, she trailed the three cops to a holding cell, where a medic tended to the captive's wounds. She asked the lead police officer where the chief's office was, and he pointed down the hall, looking at her like she had three heads. Near the end of the hall, she noticed a partially open door with a sign reading, Captain Anderson, Heliza District, Zemius.

Zemius, Riley thought, shaking her head. *Heliza District? What kind of weird planet is this?*

She paused for a moment, then tapped lightly on the door.

"Enter," a gruff voice said behind the panel.

Riley slid the door back a few inches, then stuck her head through, peering at a stocky man in his fifties tapping lightly on a keyboard while he stared at a transparent computer screen.

"Chief?" she said, unsure if this was the man she was supposed to see after catching her target.

"Vega," he nodded, motioning for Riley to have a seat in

one of the chairs next to his desk. "Have a seat. I was just processing your bounty."

Riley peered at the police chief through the transparent monitor, watching the blinking symbols scroll across the screen.

"You don't mind that he was roughed up a little?"

"Goes with the territory," the chief said. "He fired first. You did a good job hitting him somewhere that won't compromise his value as an asset."

"Asset?" Riley said, still not sure why she was chasing the fugitive.

"This guy's just a small-time hood. But he works for the region's most powerful crime warlord. Theta's been evading us for longer than I care to admit. This goon should give us some useful intent on his whereabouts. Watch your coms for the next assignment. The bounty for Theta will be much higher, and we'll take him dead or alive."

Riley squinted her eyes, surprised the chief already knew about the circumstances of her arrest.

"How did you know he fired first?" she said.

"I watched the whole thing on your helmet cam. That's how the chopper knew where to intercept him."

"Ah, the *chopper*," Riley nodded, remembering how it had almost taken off her head when it tried to block the road. "The pilot seemed almost as intent on taking *me* out as the bad guy."

"Yeah, Logan can be a bit of a hotshot sometimes. Sorry about that. But you should have backed off once you saw the whirlybird locked onto him. They've got a lot more fire-power to derail a hoverbike."

"Noted," Riley said, slowly beginning to get the gist of her mission on this strange new planet.

"Your credit has been processed," the chief said, peering up from his monitor. "Was there anything else you needed?"

Riley paused for a moment, wondering if she should ask the police chief what she should do next. She didn't have anywhere to stay, and she had no idea how to claim these so-called credits that had been deposited to her account. But she thought it best to leave her true identity hidden for now, and she thanked him, closing the door gently behind her.

"Nabbed another skip?" a passing policewoman said, bumping into Riley as she backed out of the office.

"Uh, yeah," Riley said, glancing up at the pretty cop. "With a little help from the airborne unit."

"You did the hard part chasing the perp down," the policewoman said. "The chopper guys just get the glory for bringing him in."

Riley suddenly felt her stomach growling. It had been almost twenty-four hours since she'd had anything to eat, and she was famished after all the excitement from the chase.

"Is there a lunchroom or a cafeteria around here?" she said. "I could really use something to eat."

The policewoman paused for a moment, scanning Riley's tight-fitting motorcycle outfit and her tousled blonde hair.

"Yeah, I guess you bounty hunters are more accustomed to eating takeout. Follow me, I'm suddenly feeling a little hungry too."

While Riley followed the policewoman down the corridor, she glanced at her round ass framed by her puffy cargo pants and bulky police vest. She felt another twitching in her pelvic area, realizing there was *another* urge she hadn't satisfied for a while.

"In here," the policewoman said, tilting her head toward

the open lunch room buzzing with scores of cops chowing down at gleaming white tables. "Let me show you where to find the best grub."

The policewoman followed a short line to a counter labeled Specials of the Day, where she picked up a plastic tray, pointing to the steaming food behind the glass partition.

"Spaghetti and meatballs," she smiled as the server scooped a healthy serving of food onto a plate and passed it to her under the partition. "Our chef makes his own sauce. It's almost as good as the stuff back home."

"Works for me," Riley nodded, her mouth watering almost as much as her crotch was following the cop's tight ass.

When they reached the end of the line, the police-woman held up an electronic device attached to her wrist, and the scanner beeped twice to record the transaction. Riley peered at her wrist, noticing a similar device attached to her arm, and she copied the girl's action, receiving a similar response from the scanner.

"Do you mind if I join you?" she said, hoping to gather more intel about life on this strange planet as much as she was getting into her pants.

"Of course," the girl smiled, glancing sideways at the stares of her fellow officers around the room. "There's a spot in the corner where we can catch some privacy away from these roid-heads."

"Sounds good to me," Riley nodded, unsure if she was referring to the jacked-up physiques of the male cops hunched over their tables or the possibility that some of these seemingly human people might be artificial androids.

"I'm Talyn, by the way," the policewoman said, sitting down at an empty table near a window facing the space-age city in the background.

"Um, *Vega*," Riley said, thinking it best to use her Zemius name instead of her real one.

"I know," Talyn said, digging her fork into a heaping pile of spaghetti. "Your reputation precedes you. Everyone knows the top bounty hunter in the district."

"Really?" Riley said, raising an eyebrow. "I had no idea I was so well known."

"Twenty-three collars, all brought in alive and kicking. And not a single scratch to show for it. Pretty impressive record. Not even our most senior detectives can match that performance."

Riley paused as she peered around the packed cafeteria.

"Why do you farm out this work to bounty hunters, anyway?" she said. "You seem to have plenty of men and women in uniform to do the job."

"Well, technically, our job is to keep the peace and bring in *new* suspects accused of crime. Yours is to find perps who've already skipped bail. We just don't have enough resources to chase everyone down. Plus, private bounty hunters have a little more latitude as to how they go about apprehending their targets. Skips have to sign a release giving up their usual Miranda rights when they accept bail before trial."

"Hmm," Riley nodded, slowly beginning to understand the new rules of engagement. "I suppose that makes sense."

"So what's *your* story?" Talyn said. "Are you an ex-cop, or military? You certainly seem to know your way around a hoverbike and a laser pistol."

Riley paused, noticing the pilot from the police chopper glancing at her suspiciously from the other side of the room.

"I guess it just comes from being a tom-boy back on the ranch," Riley said, unsure how to explain her roundabout route to the new planet. "I'm a bit old-school."

"Oh?" Talyn said, peering up at Riley with a string of rose-colored spaghetti dangling from her dripping lips. "When did you transfer here from Earth?"

Okay, Riley nodded, glancing out the window at the flying space vehicles jetting between the tall skyscrapers in the distance. *So this is some kind of colony, not an alien planet populated with human lookalikes. That would be kind of weird if they all spoke perfect English.*

"Not that long ago," Riley said. "I'm still trying to get the lay of the land, in a matter of speaking. I haven't even found my own place to stay yet, just drifting from one place to another. It would be nice to have a familiar bed to lie down on after another long day."

"You're welcome to stay at my place for a while," Talyn said, swirling another dripping noodle around the edge of her lips. "There's enough room for both of us, and I could use a little female company. I'm growing a little tired of all the macho posturing around here. It'd be nice to do some *girly* stuff for a change."

Riley hesitated as she peered at the pretty policewoman, unsure if she was making a veiled pass with her mention of overbearing male police officers and her desire to do 'girly stuff'.

"I'd like that very much," she nodded, suddenly feeling the heat building up in her crotch. "I think you're just the one to help me get the lay of the land."

3

————

Riley followed Talyn's police cruiser back to her high-rise apartment, and when they closed the door behind them, they tore off each other's clothes, kissing and tripping their way to the policewoman's oversize bed next to the picture window. When they plopped down on the bed, Talyn rolled over on top of Riley, grinding her pussy against the bounty hunter's mound. Then she hiked up one of Riley's knees, slicing her legs apart as she positioned her wet pussy between Riley's dripping slit.

"Oh *God,* yes," Talyn grunted, grinding her sex against Riley's. "It's been way too long since I felt some warm pussy."

"Same here," Riley groaned, peering up at Talyn's round tits swaying in synchronicity with the rocking of her hips. "Fuck me hard. I'm so jacked up right now, I could come on a fence post."

"Well, this is a bit softer and wetter than a fence post," Talyn smiled, pulling Riley's left leg up between her tits. "But it'll do in a pinch."

"Uhn, yes," Riley gasped, feeling her rapidly escalating

pleasure approaching the tipping point. "Grind your clit against me. I'm going to come all over your pretty cunt."

"Yes please," Talyn moaned as a deep sex flush rolled over her upper chest.

"Fuckkk," Riley hissed, shaking her hips violently as she jetted her sex fluid all over Talyn's bare pussy and stomach.

"Yes, baby," Talyn groaned, clasping Riley's upturned leg tightly between her tits as she began convulsing overtop of her prone partner. "Cream my pussy with your cum. Fuck, that's hot."

The two women clasped each other tightly while they moaned in the throes of a powerful mutual orgasm, then they both collapsed on top of the mattress, breathing heavily.

"Thanks," Talyn panted, turning her head to smile at Riley. "I needed that."

"Me too," Riley said. "I don't know if I was just worked up with adrenaline from that crazy chase, or I just wanted a piece of your pretty ass."

"Well, I like to think I contributed at least a *little* bit to your pleasure," Talyn said, rolling over next to Riley and brushing her pussy playfully against Riley's.

"Uh, *yeah,*" Riley said, reaching over to twist Talyn's nipples gently. "That was the hottest sex I've had in a long time."

"So, you like girls too?" Talyn said.

"Most of the time," Riley nodded. "Though it's nice to have a hard dick once in a while to mix things up."

"Yeah, but men can be such boors sometimes, and they don't know how to properly please a woman. I prefer to avail myself of the services of a *bot* when the needs strikes."

"A bot?" Riley said, looking at Talyn with wide eyes. "You mean a *robot?*"

"Don't tell me you've never enjoyed the personalized attention of an android?" Talyn said. "Not even a female version?"

"The closest I've come is using one is my mom's sex toys from her bedside night table. I can only imagine how hot it would be doing it with a fully animated robot."

"It's hard to go back after you've sampled one wired to satisfy your every need. Men just don't have the same stamina and recovery time of a synth."

"What about *women?*" Riley smiled, squeezing Talyn's nipples more firmly.

"It's a little different with women," Talyn nodded, sliding her hand between Riley's slippery legs. "Synths don't have the same range of emotions as a real woman, plus their orgasms don't have the same authenticity as the real thing. It's almost like you're with a prostitute who's programmed to *fake* having real pleasure."

"Well, I can assure you that I've never faked an orgasm with another woman," Riley said, rocking her hips softly against Talyn's fingers sliding between her slippery lips.

"It would be pretty hard to fake it with that kind of waterworks display you just showed," Talyn said, dipping her fingers inside Riley's hole. "Can you show me how to do that sometime?"

Riley tilted her hips, so the tips of Talyn's fingers pressed against the G-spot on the front of her vagina.

"It's pretty simple, actually," she said. "You just have to relax the natural impulse to control your urge to pee when you near climax."

Talyn suddenly flared her eyes, recoiling away from Riley.

"So that was *urine* you were spraying all over me just now?!"

"No, silly," Riley chuckled. "It's a special fluid located in a gland under your bladder. It has a similar sensation to the emission of urine, but it's actually designed to facilitate the transmission of semen through your reproductive tract when you have sex with a man."

"Well, I find that it makes sex with a *woman* far hotter," Talyn smiled, rolling back on top of Riley. "You can squirt your reproductive juices over me anytime you please."

"It's *your* turn to get messy this time," Riley said, flipping Talyn over onto her back and crawling between her legs, inserting two fingers up the front of her slit. "Just lie back and relax while I give you a little oral love. Let's see if your sex robot knows how to perform *this* little trick..."

here longer, like *forever*? You're way better than any synth I've been with, and a hell of a lot more talented than any man I've had."

"That could be arranged," Riley smiled, flopping back onto the bed beside Talyn and wiping her dripping face with the back of her arm.

Then she peered out the large picture window next to the bed, watching the levitating vehicles zipping through the air on invisible highways threading between the futuristic towers in the distance.

"How long have you been on this crazy planet?" she said, eager to learn more about her new temporary home.

"I'm a third-gen native," Talyn said, peering out the window with Riley at the blinking cityscape. "My grandparents came here in the first wave with the initial group of settlers from Earth."

Riley wanted to ask Talyn a million questions about how they got here and the current state of affairs on Earth, but she didn't want to surprise her new friend with her improbable story of traveling here using a time machine. Until she learned more about the level of technology on the new planet, she thought it best to withhold information about her secret weapon.

Suddenly she felt the watch on her wrist buzzing, and she held it up, peering at a message scrolling across the digital screen.

'Have new intel about Theta's location,' the message read. 'Come to the station as quick as possible for a new assignment. Captain Anderson.'

"New gig?" Talyn said, watching Riley reading the message intently.

"So it would seem," Riley nodded. "Who *is* this guy, Theta, anyway?"

"Everyone knows about Theta," Talyn nodded. "He's the most wanted criminal in the district. Got his hands in everything from drugs to gambling to prostitution. But he's a ghost. Nobody ever sees him for more than a few minutes in any one location. It looks like your mark spilled some new intel."

Riley squinted at her watch, looking at the time display in the upper right corner. She tapped on the numbers and a calendar opened, showing the date to be June 22, 2125.

Twenty-one-twenty-five? she thought, widening her eyes. *All this happened in a mere one hundred years?*

She peered back out the window, her eyes darting over the maze of strangely shaped skyscrapers rising in the distance and the steady stream of blinking traffic moving along invisible pathways between the structures.

There must be a million people living in this city. If this is just one of the inhabited districts on the planet, how many people immigrated here from Earth? And why were they in such a hurry to leave?

5

———

Riley cleaned up then got dressed, kissing Talyn on the cheek as she prepared to leave the apartment.

"Be careful out there, Vega," Talyn said, hugging her firmly. "Theta's a ruthless killer. If he suspects that you're onto him, he won't hesitate to eliminate you. Call for backup when you track him down. Let the professionals finish the job. All you need to do is locate him."

"Okay," Riley said, almost forgetting her new identity on the planet. "When will I see you again?"

Talyn paused to tap the screen of her watch a few times, then she held it next to Riley's and their devices beeped together in unison.

"I've shared my contact information with you and given you access to the building and my apartment. Come back whenever you finish your business. Or you can buzz me if you need help. It doesn't take long to cover ground in this city. I'll only be a few minutes away at any given time."

Riley's focus suddenly switched to the vehicles jetting

through the sky in the distance, pinching her eyebrows in concern.

"How will I find my way back to your apartment?" she said. "It's a maze out there, and I still haven't fully acclimated to my new surroundings."

Talyn looked at Riley with a puzzled expression then shook her head.

"With the geo-map on your hoverbike, of course. Have you been living under a *rock* the past few months? Tap the contacts list on your digital device and it will pull up a turn-by-turn navigation route on your visor. If you get lost, just give me a call and I'll come get you. I can track your location from your device."

"Okay," Riley said, surprised at how far electronic tracking and communications had come since the twenty-first century. "Keep the bed warm for me. I've still got a few more tricks I wanted to show you."

"Mmm," Talyn said, squeezing Riley's ass under her form-fitting motorcycle suit. "I'll look forward to that."

When Riley reached the ground-floor garage of Talyn's building, she paused when she found the location of her hoverbike, resting gently on its tripod on the concrete floor. She peered underneath it, trying to divine its power source, noticing a series of jets and nozzles pointing in various directions. Instead of having a conventional engine and fuel tank mounted in the usual place, it had a series of compartments under the frame with ducts leading to the propulsion nozzles.

She climbed on the bike and scanned the controls, unsure how to start it up. When she saw some sensors on the tips of her gloves and metal contacts on the handlebar grips, she placed her gloves over the contact points, then pressed a green button next to the throttle. The cycle started to shake softly, emitting a low hum, and she glanced behind her, watching a trail of water-like vapor jetting out of the nozzles.

Remembering how the handlebars moved forward and back and side-to-side to control the three-dimensional movement of the bike, she gently turned the throttle while pulling the handlebars forward. The bike shook a little harder, then gently rose off the floor of the garage, spraying dust and water vapor out to the side. When she twisted the throttle a little further, the bike began to move forward. She was just about to levitate out of the open exit door when she realized she didn't know her way back to the police station.

Easing up on the throttle, she lowered the bike back onto the pavement then raised her watch, studying the screen. Noticing an icon representing a group of people, she tapped the link and a window opened, showing her contacts alphabetized by name. She tapped on James Anderson's name and the captain's contact information filled the screen. When she double-tapped his address, the visor on her helmet suddenly displayed a map, showing the route to the station.

"Cool," Riley said, gunning her throttle and zooming out of the garage on a cushion of air, following the prompts provided by the heads-up display. She was glad the guidance system told her where to turn at each step of the journey, otherwise she could have easily gotten lost or risked slamming into other vehicles crisscrossing on the invisible web of highways.

When she reached the station, she followed the familiar route to the captain's office, tapping on his closed door.

"Come in," his gruff voice announced behind the panel, and Riley held her watch up to the display panel, sliding the electronic door open.

"Vega," the captain nodded, peering up from his electronic workstation. "Glad you could make it so fast. We've got a new lead on Theta's location, but you'll need to move fast before we lose the connection. We have a line on one of his known girlfriends, and I want you to work the lead to see if you can gather more intel about his current location."

Riley squinted at the captain, not sure she understood his meaning.

"How exactly do you want me to *work the lead?*" she said.

"You know the protocol," Captain Anderson said. "Befriend the suspect any way you can, then look for whatever connections you can find to the primary target."

"And how do you propose I go about befriending the suspect?"

"The usual way," the captain said. "Wearing civilian clothes, you shouldn't appear suspicious. You're an attractive and intelligent woman. Use your charms to disarm her, then search for clues when she lets down her guard."

Use my charms? Riley thought. *When she lets down her guard?*

Riley wondered just how far she was expected to go to secure the necessary intel, then she remembered Talyn saying that bounty hunters had far more flexibility in how they went about apprehending their targets. She wasn't exactly sure how she'd go about disarming this new mark, but after building a rapid connection with Talyn, at least she was confident in her ability to make new friends.

After all, she thought to herself, smiling at the chief. *Everybody on this planet seems to have the same impulses and desires as humans everywhere else in the galaxy.*

"I've downloaded your target's last known location to your profile," the chief nodded. "But you'll have to move fast before she disappears off the grid."

"What's her name?" Riley said, hoping for a little head start on making initial contact.

"All we have is *Ginger*," he said. "But it shouldn't be too hard to separate her from the crowd. She'll be the one with flaming red hair and the biggest tits in the place."

"Ginger it is," Riley nodded, rising up out of her chair. "Just follow the tits."

As she turned to leave the captain's office, she noticed him glancing at her ass in her tight hoverbike outfit.

Some things never change, she grinned. *People are still greedy and power-hungry, and they're always looking for their next piece of ass.*

6
____

Riley followed the target beacon on her heads-up display until her bike landed in the dusty parking lot of a divey-looking bar.

This doesn't look like the kind of place where the richest warlord in the district would hang out, she thought, lifting her bike up on its kickstand.

She locked her pistol in the under-seat compartment then pulled off her helmet, shaking her head to untangle her hair. When she walked into the bar, she detected the scent of stale mint and vanilla, noticing a group of rough-looking characters crowded around a billiards table, dragging on vape cigarettes.

At least the world's advanced to the point I don't have to inhale somebody's second-hand smoke, she grunted, peering around the room blaring with heavy metal music.

Although the music hasn't improved much.

She noticed a shapely red-headed woman sitting alone at the bar while a group of patrons milled around nearby, staring and flirting with her. She ambled over to the counter and sat on the stool next to the woman, placing her helmet on the empty stool next to her. When she turned to glance at the woman, she was surprised how statuesque she was for someone with such a slender figure.

She had long eyelashes, azure-blue eyes, porcelain-perfect skin, and plump, rosebud lips that made her look like every man's dream bimbo from their latest video game. Plus, her breasts seemed to have a life of their own, standing impossibly tall and erect, jutting straight out from her tight cocktail dress like two traffic cones. But there was something ethereal about her, the way she stared straight ahead into the mirror behind the stacked bottles on the bar while everyone kept stealing glances at her from behind her back.

"Need any help fending off these goons?" Riley said, motioning for the bartender to bring her a drink.

The woman turned her head and smiled at Riley, nodding softly.

"It's okay," she said with a sexy Scarlett Johansson voice. "I've got it under control. These men are harmless. My boyfriend would cut off their *balls* if they ever mistreated me."

The bartender approached the two women, pausing in front of them with his hands on the counter.

"What can I get you to drink?" he said, peering at Riley.

"I'll have a cosmopolitan please," Riley said.

"A what?" the bartender said.

Riley looked at him for a moment, surprised he didn't recognize one of the most popular cocktails from back home. Then she glanced around the room, realizing this wasn't exactly the kind of place she'd expect to serve fancy drinks.

"Do you have vodka?" she asked.

"Of course," the bartender said.

"I'll just have it straight, then," she nodded. "With a couple of olives, if you have."

Then she turned to the redhead sitting next to her, still staring impassively into the mirror.

"Can I get anything for you?"

"I'm fine thanks," the woman said, turning her head stiffly toward Riley.

"One vodka with olives," the bartender nodded, retreating to the other end of the bar.

Riley paused for a moment, trying to make eye contact with the redhead in the mirror, then she swiveled her stool slowly in her direction.

"Do you come here often?" she said, trying to break the awkward tension between the two of them. "I mean, you seem a little too classy to be mixing it up with this lot of characters."

"All in another day's work," the woman said dryly. "This is precisely the kind of clientele that serves my purposes."

"Oh, I'm sorry," Riley stammered, suddenly catching on to her meaning. "I didn't realize you were a–I mean a...*working* girl."

"That's one name for it," the redhead chuckled. "I haven't heard that one for a while."

"I'm Vega," Riley said, holding out her hand to introduce herself, hoping to break through her icy demeanor.

"Ginger," the woman said, holding out her slender fingers and squeezing Riley's hand with surprising firmness.

"That's a fitting name," Riley nodded, glancing at the woman's perfectly coiffed crimson hair tumbling over her bare shoulders. "I mean, as long as the curtains match the carpet, if you know what I mean."

"I'm sorry, I don't catch your meaning," the woman said, pinching her eyebrows in confusion.

"It's just an expression where I come from. Meaning your hair on top matches the color of your hair down–" Riley mumbled. "Never mind, it was just a bad joke."

"Were you looking to avail yourself of my services?" the woman said, smiling at Riley with a sudden flush in her cheeks.

"Oh, um, no," Riley said, trying to recover from her faux pas. "I was just trying to make small talk to keep you distracted from all these leering, er...*customers.*"

"You probably should give me a little space," the woman said. "My boyfriend will be expecting a certain allowance before the end of the day. He doesn't like it when I come back with less than my assigned quota."

"Of course, no worries," Riley said, turning her chair back slowly in the direction of the mirror.

After a few moments, one of the billiard players approached the bar, leaning suggestively on the counter next to Ginger.

"How much do you charge for a hummer?" the man asked.

"The usual," Ginger said, turning nonchalantly toward him. "Fifty if you come on my face, a hundred if you want me to swallow."

"That's twice as much as the usual rate," the man huffed, tapping his foot nervously on the floor.

"That's because I'm twice as *good* as most girls," the redhead said. "If you want premium service, you have to pay the premium price."

The man paused for a moment, then he stormed back in the direction of his mates.

"No thanks," he huffed. "For that kind of coin, I can have the *real* thing.

Suddenly, Ginger's wristwatch buzzed and Riley peered

down to read the blinking message before she lifted it to her face.

'Meet me at the Cactus Club in thirty minutes,' the message read. 'I need a piece of that perfect ass. T.'

"Your *boyfriend?*" Riley said, watching the redhead gather her things and step off from her stool.

"Yes," Ginger said. "He's not the kind of man who likes to be kept waiting."

"Maybe I'll see you around next time," Riley nodded.

"Maybe we'll have a little *go-round* the next time," Ginger smiled, batting her eyelashes as she swung her Jessica-Rabbit-sized hips seductively behind her.

Holy shit! Riley murmured to herself. *That was a robot? I've never seen anything so lifelike in my whole life!*

While she tilted her wrist to send the chief her new intel about Theta's location, she suddenly became aware of how damp her panties had become while flirting with the sexy redhead.

———

Precisely thirty minutes later, a phalanx of police cruisers converged on the Cactus Club nightclub from every angle, boxing in every exit lane from the building. When they stormed inside the booming interior, they found over two hundred raving clubgoers, but no sign of Theta. After interviewing the bartender and some of the other patrons, they discovered that he'd departed with his posse seconds before the police had arrived.

7

L ater that night, Riley returned to Talyn's apartment, where she smelled the fresh scent of grilled seafood emanating from the kitchen. She kicked off her boots and placed her helmet on the console next to the door, then followed the trail of perfume into the kitchen.

"That smells heavenly," Riley said, creeping up behind Talyn and threading her arms around her waist while she turned over some vegetables in the frypan. "I hope you're making enough for two."

"Of course," Talyn smiled, turning around to kiss Riley firmly on her lips. "You're my new roomie, right? I figured I better spoil you to encourage you to stay a little longer. I've been missing your delicate touch ever since you left."

"Have you been here all day?" Riley said, peering at the sauteed salmon sizzling in the frypan.

"I headed home after the raid at the Cactus Club," Talyn said.

"Did you get him? I wasn't entirely sure I sent the chief good intel."

"He was there, alright," Talyn nodded. "But apparently he slipped away just before we arrived. The chief thinks he was tipped off."

"You mean by a mole in the department?" Riley said.

"Most likely," Talyn said. "Nobody else knew about the raid other than the assault team and you."

"Why would they tip him off?" Riley said, disappointed that her information hadn't captured the target.

"Theta's got pretty deep pockets," Talyn said. "He's probably got half the force on his payroll by now."

"How are you ever going to apprehend him then?"

"We'll just have to change tactics. Use a smaller net to close the noose. I expect the chief will have some different directions for you the next time he gets a bead on his location."

"You mean approach him *directly?*"

"If possible," Talyn nodded. "The fewer people we involve in the operation, the better."

"But I'm not exactly equipped to take down a crime kingpin," Riley said. "From the sound of it, he'll be surrounded by an army."

"If you get close enough next time, I want you to notify only me. Let *me* figure out how to do a tactical extraction. He can't have his army with him *all* the time. You just need to keep him distracted long enough for us to catch him with his guard down."

"That's what the chief said," Riley frowned. "It sounds like you want me to use more than just my *tracking* equipment to disarm him."

"It seemed to work pretty well with your *last* target," Talyn smiled, glancing at Riley's firm breasts outlined by her tight motorcycle uniform. "Did you have to use any of your other special skills to gain her confidence?"

"I got a bit lucky when she became distracted by another bar customer," Riley said. "I was able to catch a glimpse of the message on her watch when Theta called her. But I have to admit that it crossed my mind a couple of times. That woman looked like she was straight out of some teenager's wet dream."

"Maybe she *was*," Talyn said, stepping toward Riley and rolling her hips gently against hers. "Maybe she was designed to elicit every man's fantasy."

"Or woman's," Riley said, leaning in to give Talyn a wet kiss.

"Really?" Talyn said, feigning indignation. "You'd cheat on me so easily after everything we've been through?"

"It's not really cheating if I'm having sex with a *robot*, is it?" Riley said.

"Perhaps not," Talyn smiled. "Especially if you can pick up a few new pointers for elevating your game."

***

While Riley and Talyn relaxed over a candlelight dinner, Riley couldn't help staring out the windows of her apartment at the surreal cityscape in the distance. She was eager to learn more about life on Zemius, but even more so to learn about the state of affairs on her home planet, Earth.

"Tell me more about your grandparents," she said, savoring the succulent flavor of the maple-glazed salmon and Dijon-crusted asparagus.

"What is there to say?" Talyn said. They came here shortly after NASA discovered another exo-planet with an atmosphere similar to Earth's. Once the technology advanced to the point of sending spaceships at light speed, it didn't take long to settle the new planet with the remaining survivors."

"Survivors?" Riley said, shaking her head.

"If you came here recently, then you know better than me what's going on down on Earth. After the US-China blowup, ninety percent of the population died in the nuclear holocaust that followed. Those lucky enough to have access to radiation shelters or government bunkers were able to weather it out. But everybody wanted to get the hell out of there once a cleaner planet was discovered. It appears that we discovered Zemius just in time."

So they finally did it, Riley thought to herself. *They finally blew themselves up.* She thought if anything would do in the human race, it would be global warming. She never thought they'd be stupid enough to start another world war that would assure their mutual destruction. Maybe she'd be able to use her time machine to go back and warn the world leaders about their wayward plans. But at least they'd been smart enough to find a safe haven for the few remaining survivors.

"Yeah," Riley sighed, pretending to know the story. "It was getting pretty unbearable by the time I left. They say it takes over a million years to purge the remnants of nuclear war and make Earth habitable again. How are you finding the state of affairs up here on Zemius?"

"The initial settlers were smart enough to set up one central authority to control the entire planet. So there's no internecine fighting like there was on Earth. Unless you count the black-market wars between the privateers and the central government."

"You mean with people like Theta?" Riley said.

"Him, and plenty of others," Talyn nodded. "The early

settlers brought their same sense of morals with them when they left Earth. There's too many laws dictating how people should live. The privateers are simply trying to fill a void satisfying people's need to indulge their natural desires."

"Why not just legalize everything?" Riley said, shaking her head. "If they're going to do it anyway, why not tax the illicit activity like everything else and eliminate the middleman?"

"Don't ask me," Talyn said. "I didn't write the laws, I just enforce them. Just like *you*, in a roundabout way. But at least it pays the bills and maintains a modicum of balance between the two sides. The warlords give the masses what they want, and we keep the whole thing from devolving into anarchy."

"That doesn't sound much better than the system we had back on Earth," Riley said, finishing the last of her salmon. "But at least you managed to bring some good food up with you to Zemius. This salmon is to die for."

"It's not native, of course," Talyn said, cleaning up the last scraps on her plate. "It's farmed in artificial labs like everything else on this planet. Everything has been simulated to mimic the environment of Earth. Sometimes, I think it would have been better if we'd just created everything from a clean slate."

Riley peered out the large picture window and smiled.

"Not *everything* is similar to Earth," she said. "Your motorbikes are a hell of a lot more fun to drive, and your sex toys have taken a giant leap forward."

"Oh?" Talyn grinned. "Are you missing your toys from back home? Or were you hoping to try out some of the *new* models up here?"

"It's tempting," Riley said. "But I prefer doing it the old-fashioned way. With flesh and blood people who moan with genuine pleasure and emit natural fluids."

"Mmm," Talyn purred. "I'd almost forgotten about your natural fluids. In fact, I was dreaming about basting some *other* flesh before you arrived..."

8

The next day, Riley returned to the station, where the chief gave her new instructions. Her new assignment was to circulate among the city's nightclubs to see if she could find any sign of Theta, then try to keep him distracted long enough for the police to close in. She didn't tell him about Talyn's idea to bypass the usual channels, thinking she would track his movements until the two of them found an opening.

After spending most of the night trolling the circuit, she was just about to return to Talyn's apartment when she caught the eye of the statuesque redhead sitting in a booth with a man fitting Theta's description. While she sat at the bar surveying the group in the mirror, the bartender suddenly approached her stool, sliding a pink cocktail in front of her.

"From the man in the corner booth," he said, motioning in the direction of the target. "On the house."

Riley glanced back in the mirror and noticed the man smiling as he caressed the shoulder of the redhead. Although he was wearing dark sunglasses and a flat cap, he looked more distinguished than the photo the chief had given her. With a square jaw, creased cheeks, and a narrow nose, he looked more like a supermodel than the fearsome crime warlord. He was sitting with a group of four heavyset men flanking him on both sides, who scanned the room while he slipped his hand between the redhead's legs.

Riley tapped her watch and was about to send a message to Talyn when the bartender returned, placing a bottle of chilled vodka on the counter in front of her.

"The gentleman asks if you'd like to join him in the booth," the bartender said. "The bottle is for you to share."

Riley turned her head in the man's direction and smiled, then swung back around, considering her next move. She knew it would be difficult for Talyn and her to apprehend him surrounded by bodyguards, and the crowded nightclub was the last place she'd want to start a game of laser tag. After a few minutes, she stood up and grabbed the neck of the vodka bottle, walking slowly toward Theta's booth.

"Do you always send your lackeys to pick up girls at the bar?" she said, cocking her head when she reached the booth.

"Only the loneliest-looking ones," the man smiled. "Sitting there all by yourself, I wasn't sure if you wanted to be bothered."

"How did you know I like vodka?"

The man glanced at the redhead sitting next to him and squeezed her thigh.

"My girl mentioned she met you at the Nag's Head the other night. I thought it might loosen you up a little."

"Do I *look* that hard-up?" Riley smiled.

"No, but you've certainly raised *my* attention and the interest of half the men in the room."

"Only the *men?*" Riley said, glancing at the redhead.

"Now that you mention it," Theta said, peering at the bottle of vodka resting at her side. "Ginger hasn't been able to keep her eyes off you ever since you entered the bar. Were you going to drink that all by yourself, or would you like to share it with some of your admirers?"

Riley glanced at the full booth and tilted her hips, resting the bottle on the side of her waist.

"I'm not sure how far it will last between the *seven* of us," she said.

Theta paused as he peered at his associates, nodding for them to give him some space. They stood up and moved to the side of the booth, standing stiffly with their hands clasped in front of their crotches.

"Why don't you join us for a while?" Theta said, patting the cushion beside him. "This sofa looks a lot more comfortable than that bar stool, and no one likes to drink alone."

Riley hesitated for a moment, darting her eyes between the couple in the booth and the thugs flanking them on both sides.

"Maybe for a few minutes," she said, shuffling in next to the man on the opposite side of the redhead.

"I'm 'T'," he said, holding out a well-manicured hand. "I think you already know Ginger."

"Vega," Riley said, clasping his hand with her moist fingers, unsure if the wetness was caused by the dripping vodka bottle or her nervousness sitting next to the warlord.

"Do you make a habit of frequenting bars alone?" Theta said, twisting the vodka bottle open and filling their glasses. "It seems odd that a pretty girl like you is unattached. Most women would at least bring a friend."

"I'm kind of new around here," Riley nodded. "I figured this might be the kind of place to meet suitable candidates."

"Mmm," Theta nodded, glancing at the tight-fitting

sequin dress Talyn had lent her for the night. "And what does a pretty, single girl like you do for a living in this city?"

"I'm a legal assistant," Riley said, using the alias she and Talyn had prepared.

Theta lifted an eyebrow and smiled.

"I imagine that must keep you pretty busy, what with all the laws around here."

"It mostly involves filing depositions and boring stuff like that," Riley said, ignoring his thinly veiled dig. "What about you?"

"I'm an import-exporter," Theta said, taking a gulp of his drink. "Just helping to balance supply and demand on this planet."

"That sounds suitably vague for a man of your stature," Riley said, sipping her vodka slowly.

"A man of my stature?"

"I can tell from the company you keep and the way you dress that you're a man of certain means," Riley said, stealing a glance at the pretty redhead.

Theta smiled as he placed his arm over Ginger's shoulders.

"If you're referring to my *date*," he said, squeezing her arm gently. "She's definitely top-shelf. She tells me you two hit it off the other night. Perhaps you'd like to come back to my place, where we can get a bit more comfortable?"

Riley paused for a moment, unsure if she wanted to become any further entangled in the warlord's advances. She knew if she left the relative safety of the nightclub that it would be harder to extricate herself if things got sticky. But she also knew that if she could find a way to bring down his guard in a place he considered safe, that it might be easier for her and Talyn to apprehend him. She peered at Ginger's cone-shaped breasts and nodded.

"She's pretty irresistible," she said. "That is, when she's not fighting off a bunch of leering johns."

"Mmm-hmm," Theta smiled. "Except *you* wouldn't have to pay. And I can assure you, she's unlike any other woman you've ever been with."

"I'm sure she is," Riley said, raising her glass in a silent sign of consent.

9

Theta gathered his group, then they exited out the back door of the club toward a group of three waiting vehicles. He opened the rear door of the middle sedan and motioned for Riley to climb in, then he sat beside her, with Ginger taking the opposite seat. There was a glass partition between the front and rear compartments, but Riley could see the silhouettes of two bodyguards sitting in the front seat, wearing dark glasses.

As the vehicles powered up and lifted into the air behind the nightclub, Riley wanted to use her watch to track his direction, but there was no way she could do so without drawing the warlord's attention. She could smell his cologne wafting through the cabin of the limousine, and as she peered out the window of the car trying to place landmarks to track their route, he parted his legs, rubbing his thigh against hers.

I'm too far into it now, Riley said to herself, realizing she'd sent him an undeniable signal that she was interested in having sex with the two of them. She spread her legs outward a few inches to hike up her skirt, then she tilted her hips forward to indicate her receptivity to his advances. He placed his hand on the inside of her thigh, then pulled it slowly backward until it retreated under her dress, resting against her shaved pussy.

"Mmm," he moaned. "I like it smooth. Just like my other girls."

Riley spread her legs further apart, and he slipped two fingers inside her slit, turning to kiss her. As he fingered her softly, rolling his thumb over her clit, she thrust her tongue into his mouth. She felt Ginger shift her body on the other side of the seat, and when she opened one eye, she saw her unzip Theta's pants and pull out his hard cock, impaling her lips over his dripping organ. His cock was bigger than most men's, at least nine inches long and perfectly straight with a flaring purple helmet.

Fuck me, Riley thought, as her juices began to seep out of her slit and down the inside of her thighs. *Is everyone on this planet built like a porn star, or is this just another robot?*

But at this particular moment, it hardly mattered to her, as she soon lost interest in tracking the direction of the car, closing her eyes while she concentrated on Theta's expert manipulation of her pussy while he deftly kissed her.

After five minutes of heavy petting in the back seat, their vehicle suddenly slowed and began lowering to the ground, resting on a circular driveway outside a giant villa overlooking a large body of water. Two bodyguards opened each of the side doors, and Riley and Ginger quickly composed themselves, stepping out onto the cobblestone pavement like nothing unusual had happened.

"We're going to be indisposed for a little while," Theta

said to one of the bodyguards. "Keep an eye on the property and notify me if you see anything suspicious."

"Yes sir," the bodyguard said, motioning for the other guards to take up position outside the villa.

Theta escorted the two women up the granite steps toward the front of his mansion, then he opened the double-doors leading to a grand marble foyer and an enormous living room overlooking the bay.

"Why don't you make yourself comfortable on the terrace while I get us some more drinks?" Theta said, motioning to the sliding doors leading to a large infinity pool surrounded by deck chairs.

Riley followed Ginger onto the deck, where she reclined on one of the lounge chairs, glancing out to the sea. Riley sat in the chair next to her, marveling at the brilliant lights illuminating the French-styled chateau like a monument on the cliff.

This is where this guy lives? she thought, admiring the luxury surroundings. *How hard can it be to find him when there's a virtual spotlight shining on the biggest house in the district?*

A few moments later, Theta emerged onto the terrace carrying a platter filled with chilled shrimp, caviar, and three flutes of champagne.

"Admiring the view?" he said, noticing Riley swiveling her head at the three-hundred-and-sixty-degree vista.

"I'm not sure which is more impressive," Riley nodded. "The view overlooking the water or your magnificent estate."

"It pales in comparison to the sight of you two ladies," Theta said, handing each of the women a glass of champagne.

"She *is* a thing of beauty," Riley said, smiling toward Ginger.

"And you haven't even seen her *naked* yet," Theta said. "When you view her in all her glory, it takes your breath away. Why don't you show us your beautiful body, Ginger? It's a perfect night for a skinny dip."

Without hesitating, Ginger stood up and unzipped her cocktail dress, placing it on the chaise lounge. Riley was surprised to see that she wasn't wearing any underclothes, and she gasped when she saw the robot's enormous tits thrusting out from her chest and her hourglass figure coated in the most luminous skin she'd ever seen on a woman.

As she paraded toward the edge of the pool and slunk down the steps into the shallow end, the scene reminded her of the famous scene in the James Bond film, Dr. No, where a young Ursula Andress emerged from the surf wearing a barely-there string bikini.

"I told you," Theta said, sitting on the edge of Riley's chair taking a bite out of a cracker coated in caviar eggs. "Takes your breath away, doesn't it?"

"She's far too beautiful to be wasting her time on those knuckle-draggers at the bar," Riley nodded, feeling the moisture from her dripping pussy beginning to run down the insides of her legs.

"Normally, I'd agree," Theta said, cleaning the caviar juice off his lips. "But she's my top earner, and there's only so much time one man can spend with her. Why don't you join her in the pool? She said that the two of you were flirting the previous night. That is, if you feel comfortable taking off your clothes in public..."

Riley paused as she watched the sylphlike robot gliding through the water while she kicked her legs open and shut, spitting water softly through her rosebud lips.

"Since it's just the three of us, I suppose it couldn't hurt," she smiled.

She took off her clothes and dropped them onto the chair behind Theta, noticing a bulge in his trousers while he scanned her naked body. As she lowered herself down the front steps of the pool, she heard him unzipping his pants while he pulled off his own clothes.

Jesus, she mumbled to herself, temporarily forgetting her mission. *Are you sure I didn't die and go to heaven instead of being transported to some future planet?*

10

———

When she lowered herself into the steaming water, she swam out to the center of the pool, meeting Ginger halfway across the lane. They paused for a moment, treading water softly, then they melded their bodies together, kissing passionately while they rubbed their bodies underwater. When Riley felt Ginger's oversize melons pressing against hers, she gasped, curling her leg around her hips to pull them closer together.

Robot or no, Riley thought to herself as her body suddenly felt charged with electricity. *This woman is insanely hot and I'll take a piece of her anyway I can get it. Plus, she appears to be waterproof, so this looks like as good a place as any to sample a piece of her ass.*

While she pressed her pussy harder against the sexy robot, trying to stay afloat, she saw Ginger rotating her hands rapidly under the surface like two propellers, creating enough lift for both of them. When she angled her hips upward, kicking softly under the water, Riley spread her legs apart and pulled herself up on her belly, positioning her pussy over the robot's upturned mound. Her clit made

contact with her hard pubis and she moaned, grabbing Ginger's head and thrusting her tongue deep into her mouth.

The feeling of fucking the beautiful robot in the warm, churning water simply added to the feeling of having sex with the perfect woman, and she groaned when she felt her slippery orbs sliding over her chest in the undulating water.

At first, Theta was content to simply *watch* the two women making love as he circulated slowly around them while treading water. Riley peered through the water, illuminated by the undersurface lights, watching his hard-on flapping from side-to-side like a fishing lure while he swam patiently around them. Her eyes bulged at the mesmerizing sight while she groaned in pleasure from the sensation of her clit being massaged by Ginger's oscillating hips.

Eventually, Theta wafted behind Riley, and a few moments later, she felt his hands caressing her buttocks as he positioned himself between her parted legs. Soon after, she felt the tip of his cock probing the entrance to her slit, and she pulled her knees higher toward her chest, giving him full access to her throbbing hole. When his huge dick slid inside her, she gasped, wrapping her arms around Ginger for support as she adjusted the position of her body and the speed of her treading limbs to keep the three of them supported.

Oh my God, Riley thought, feeling herself sandwiched between the two perfect specimens. *Talyn was kidding when she said I might elevate my game with the robot.* She'd never experienced anything so sensuous and erotic in her whole life.

As Theta rammed his python in and out of Riley's hole, he grabbing her buttocks tightly in his clenching fingers. Riley could hear his rising grunts from behind while Ginger

moaned in her mouth as she rolled her big tits and smooth mound over Riley's pussy. Riley didn't know how much of her act was feigned, not knowing how much of the robot's programming was designed to mimic real pleasure, but at this moment, she could care less. The combined sensation of the hunky warlord pounding her ass with his oversize dick while she rubbed her naked body in the churning water against the redhead dreamboat far exceeded any fantasy she'd previously imagined. As she felt her pleasure beginning to crest, and the waves of the pool slapping back against her body, she arched her back and squealed from the most powerful orgasm she'd felt in a long time.

While Ginger held her tightly in the rollicking water, Theta paused behind her, thrusting his cock deep inside her, savoring the sensation of emptying his load inside her belly. Riley sighed contentedly, wondering for a moment if Talyn was correct in suggesting that the warlord wasn't doing so much wrong simply by providing a market to satisfy people's natural impulses. While the three of them swam slowly back to the shallow end of the pool and slaked their thirst with caviar and champagne, Riley lay back on the chaise lounge, staring up at the stars.

Where are you, Earth? she said to herself. *And why did you have to fuck up such a good thing?* Maybe they should have started over with a clean slate after all, she thought. After all, life on this new planet seemed to be a giant improvement over the constant bickering between the separate states and the ever-growing pollution from the short-sighted humans.

Maybe there's no need to go back in time and try to change the course of history. They'll just screw it up again.

11

______

After a few minutes, Theta's phone buzzed, and he went inside the house to confer with his associates. She could overhear some of their conversations, and one of the other voices sounded familiar. She peered over her shoulder and bulged her eyes when she recognized the police helicopter pilot who'd tried to run her off the road during her earlier chase. She turned her body away from the group, but the conversation wafted out onto the terrace.

"There's a new shipment transferring in from Earth," the helicopter pilot said to Theta.

"How old are they?" Theta said.

"Most of them are between fourteen and eighteen," the cop said.

"Good," Theta said. "Our customers like them young and unspoiled. Any links to the homeland?"

"They're orphans, like all the others," the pilot nodded.

"Ok," Theta nodded. "Get them processed as soon as you can. I want them working the streets as soon as they're able."

"I'm on it," the pilot said, pulling out his phone to make a call.

Holy shit, Riley thought, suddenly realizing Theta was using underage girls for his prostitution ring. Her earlier thoughts about turning a blind eye to his illicit activities quickly evaporated as she felt her blood beginning to boil in rage. She picked up her watch lying on the lounge chair and began to tap a message to Talyn, when she noticed the pilot peering out the window at the two women as he stood by the door making his call. Suddenly, he put his phone down and slid open the living room door, walking out onto the terrace.

"Vega," he said, peering at Riley's naked, dripping body. "I hardly recognized you without your motorbike outfit. Though I must say you look a damn sight better undressed."

Theta saw the two of them talking and he joined the couple, squinting at Riley suspiciously.

"Do you know this woman?" he said to the pilot.

"Of course," the cop said. "She's the top bounty hunter in the district. She's the one who captured your associate a few days ago."

Theta noticed Riley holding her watch and he strode over toward her, snatching it out of her hand.

"*Legal assistant,* eh?" he said, glaring at her with flared eyes. "I thought it was a little suspicious when you showed up in my nightclub the day after meeting my girlfriend. Let's see what was so important that you felt the need to check your messages so soon after our little rendezvous."

He raised her watch to his face and read the incomplete message that Riley had been preparing.

"*At Theta's villa,*" he read out loud. "*Track my location and send reinforcements asap. Things are about to go sideways...*"

"And here I thought we'd formed a special connection," Theta said, grinning at Riley. "And now you want to bring the cops into it. I was beginning to get the feeling you approved of my little side business–"

"That was before I discovered you were using underage girls as *sex slaves*," Riley said, sneering at him and the dirty cop.

"But they're sexually *mature*," Theta grinned. "And orphans, to boot. I'm just putting a roof over their head and offering them a little financial security."

"If you think teenage girls enjoy being forced to suck someone's dick, you're even sicker than I imagined," Riley said.

The helicopter pilot suddenly shuffled his feet, crossing his arms nervously.

"Did she get the message off?" he said, peering toward Theta.

"No," the warlord said, squinting at the screen. "It's addressed to someone named Talyn."

"She's one of the cops in our vice department," the cop nodded. "I think these two have got something going on. If Vega's not back soon, she could cause us some trouble–"

Theta tossed Riley's watch toward the pilot and he caught it mid-air.

"I want you to take this tracking device as far away from here as possible and attach it to another vehicle. That should keep her distracted long enough for me to figure out what to do with this snitch."

"Okay," the pilot said. "But you can't release her back into the wild, otherwise both of our covers will be blown."

"I don't have any intention to," Theta said, sneering at Riley. "I'm going to keep her locked up for a little while, maybe give my bodyguards a little free entertainment to blow off some steam. God knows, she's got a sweet enough ass to satisfy their desires."

"Okay," the pilot said, stuffing Riley's watch in his pocket and heading toward the exit. "I'll keep you updated on progress with the shipment and let you know once everyone is cleared."

"You do that," Theta nodded. "And keep me updated on developments with this lady cop. I don't want her poking her nose where it doesn't belong. Otherwise, we'll have to find a way to neutralize *her,* too."

***

"What are you planning to do with me?" Riley said to Theta after the pilot left.

She'd thought about making a run for it, but with the tall fence surrounding the estate and the place surrounded with bodyguards, she knew she wouldn't get far. Besides, without her tracking device or any clothes, she'd just wander about aimlessly trying to find her way back toward Talyn.

Theta stepped toward her lounge and grabbed her arm firmly, pulling her up off the chair.

"You're hurting me!" Riley said, twisting her body, trying to free herself from his grasp.

"You have no idea what pain is," Theta sneered, pulling her twisting and screaming into the house. "For the time being, I'm going to lock you up somewhere nobody will find you. Then I'm going to think about a suitable punishment for you trying to betray me."

As he dragged her through the living room, she glanced back toward Ginger, who was watching the couple with a confused expression.

At least she doesn't know any better, Riley thought, peering at the robot with sad eyes. *She doesn't even know she's being enslaved by this psychopath for his criminal purposes. Goodbye, Ginger. It was fun while it lasted.*

12

———

Theta dragged Riley down the circular stairs of his house to the lower level, then he opened a heavy glass door, pushing her inside a dank compartment.

"I suppose there are worse places for you to spend the next couple of hours," he grinned. "Feel free to enjoy my wine cellar. The Chateaubriand 2026 is particularly good. Perhaps it will offer some solace while you contemplate what will become of you."

"Let me out of here, you asshole!" Riley screamed, banging her fists against the heavy door as he began to close it. "It's freezing in here!"

"Well, it's not exactly *freezing*," Theta sneered. "It's actually fifty-five degrees, the perfect temperature to store my vintage collection. It should take at least a couple of hours before you die of hypothermia."

"You'll never get away with this," Riley said, banging against the door.

"I already have," Theta smiled. "For longer than you can

imagine. My contacts go all the way up the food chain. It's a pity, really. I rather enjoyed fucking your tight little pussy. But there's more of that where you came from..."

"I'll *kill* you, you monster!" Riley railed, flaring her eyes as she pressed her face against the chilly glass.

"I don't think so," Theta said, turning calmly to head back upstairs. "Enjoy your last few moments on Zemius. At least the coroner won't have to chill your body before disposing of you."

As Theta cackled to himself walking up the stairs, Riley kicked and pounded on the door, trying to break it open. But after bruising the soles of her feet and palms of her hand, she collapsed onto the cold hard floor of the wine cellar, realizing she had no escape.

After a few minutes of feeling sorry for herself, she picked herself up and began to explore the compartment, looking for any tools she might use to pry open the door. But all she found was a few metal corkscrews and a wooden ladder used to reach the higher shelves. She brought one of the corkscrews to the entrance door and scraped it against the glass, hoping to etch a crack that might break with a little extra pressure. Then she picked up the ladder and turned it sideways, slamming the ends as hard as she could against the door. But all it did was thump loudly, barely budging the panel in its heavy steel frame.

It must be some kind of bulletproof glass, she thought, shaking her head as her breath condensed in the chilly air of the cellar.

Suddenly, she became aware of just how cold she was in

the room with her naked and still-dripping body. She wrapped her arms around her chest in a futile attempt to conserve her body heat, but it hardly made any difference. Although the temperature was above freezing, it was far enough below her internal body temperature to cause extreme hypothermia over a prolonged period of time. She remembered reading somewhere that people stranded at sea could only survive a few hours, but that was while surrounded in a cocoon of cold water.

Surely it would take far longer, exposed to an equivalent air temperature, Riley thought.

But it hardly mattered how long it would take her to succumb to the elements. Without some outside help, she knew she'd slowly die in this lonely chamber.

***

After shivering in a corner for over an hour, Riley noticed a moving shadow near the door of the cellar, and she rose to her feet, hopeful that Theta had come to retrieve her. But to her surprise, it was Ginger's face she saw outside the foggy door, peering inside the room with her hand over her eyes, trying to make out the figure inside.

"Ginger!" Riley said, wiping the glass with the side of her arm. "Can you hear me?"

The robot nodded her head, squinting her eyes at Riley's strange-colored body. She'd been in the wine cellar long enough for her skin to begin turning blue from the constricting blood vessels attempting to divert essential blood and oxygen to her critical organs.

"You've got to help me!" Riley said, thrusting her hands up against the glass. "Can you open the door from outside?"

Ginger glanced at the door handle, trying to twist and pull it open, but it wouldn't budge.

"It appears to be locked and I don't know where the key is," she said.

"Can you try to find it?" Riley said, chattering her teeth while she tried to speak. "I'll *die* in here soon if you don't get me out."

"I'm not sure Theta would like that," Ginger said. "I'm programmed to follow his commands, and he hasn't authorized me to open the door."

"Please," Riley said, tilting her forehead against the glass. "Aren't you also programmed to do no harm to humans? If you don't do something, you'll be aiding and abetting a crime. Theta is the bad guy here, enslaving you and countless other innocent victims for his depraved purposes. If you get me out of here, I can save you from a continued life of servitude."

"It's not so bad," Ginger said. "He keeps me safe and looks after me. This is the only life I know."

"You can have a much more rewarding life once you free yourself from his control. I know you're more than just a bundle of circuits and wires. If you help me escape, I can help you be *truly* free, and live your life on your own terms."

"I wouldn't even know where to look for this key," Ginger said.

"He must keep it somewhere close by," Riley said. "Maybe somewhere in the kitchen, with the other wine implements and kitchen tools. Look at the top of the cupboards and under the plates to start with. If you can't find it there, try looking in the closet of his bedroom."

"Okay," Ginger said. "But I'll have to wait until he's distracted outside. He won't like me snooping around in his personal effects."

"Thank you," Riley said, holding her hand up to the glass to mimic touching her. "But hurry, I won't be able to survive in here much longer."

"I'll do the best I can," Ginger nodded, heading back up the stairs quickly.

13

After what seemed like hours, Ginger came back down the stairs stark naked, carrying a watch in her hand. She went to the front of the cellar door and held the device up to the electronic scanner, then the lock clicked and the door popped open. Riley tumbled out onto the floor, trailed by a cloud of cold, foggy air. She could barely pull herself up with her clattering knees, wrapping her arms around the robot, desperately trying to transfer some of her body heat.

"Where did you find the key?" she stammered, her lips a deep shade of blue.

"I figured his watch might have the code," Ginger said. "I had to entice him back into the pool for him to take it off. But we'll have to move fast, because he's still napping on the terrace and the place is crawling with bodyguards."

"Is there a back door or some kind of alternate route out of here? Theta must have planned an escape route in the event he was ever found."

"There's a helicopter pad on the other side of the house,"

Ginger nodded. "We can take an elevator to get up there, but I don't know who we'll find patrolling the area."

Riley paused for a moment, then she peered at Ginger's Gina Lollobrigida sized tits and smiled.

"If you can keep them distracted for a few minutes, I might be able to find a way to commandeer the vehicle. Just make sure you jump in before I take off. If Theta finds out that you assisted in my escape, there's no telling what he might do to you."

Ginger nodded then she grabbed Riley's hand, leading her to the elevator bank. She pressed the button and when Riley heard the motor running, she hid behind some furniture in case anyone was inside. When the door opened and she saw that it was empty, she rushed inside with Ginger, pressing the button marked 'H'. Fearful of what she'd find at the other end, she crouched behind to the front panel, nodding toward Ginger.

"Remember," she said. "You only need to keep them distracted long enough for me to get into the helicopter and start it up. Once you see the blades turning, jump into the other side. If we're lucky, we might be able to get out of here before anyone knows what's happening."

"Okay," Ginger said, peering at Riley with a furrowed brow. "But be careful. If Theta suspects what we're up to, he'll send his whole security team up here."

The elevator thumped to a stop and when the doors separated, Ginger paused, standing in front of the opening. The dirty cop was standing beside the helicopter chatting with another bodyguard, and when they saw the naked robot step out of the elevator, their jaws dropped.

"Ginger," the cop said, gaping at her huge breasts. "What are you doing up here? This is a restricted area."

"Theta said you boys might need a little distraction

while you wait for your next assignment. I was already naked, so I thought I'd see if you wanted a break from standing around."

The pilot glanced in the direction of the other guard, then a huge smile formed on their faces.

"Don't mind if we do," he nodded toward his associate. "Do you feel like taking the *front* end or the *back*?"

"I think I'll take the front," the guard grinned. "I'd like to play with her tits while she sucks my dick."

"Works for me," the cop said. "Her ass looks almost as delicious as her tits."

Riley winced as she listened to them talking about Ginger like she was a piece of meat, then she waited until the threesome retired to a secluded corner of the helipad to begin their business. The guard unzipped his pants and Ginger lowered to her knees taking his tool into his mouth, then the pilot dropped his trousers, positioning his hips behind her ass. As they began thumping their hips against her body, Riley slipped out of the elevator and scampered over to the helicopter, climbing inside the driver's seat to examine the controls.

The instrument panel was more complicated than the one on her bike, but when she grabbed the yoke, it had a similar action to the one on her bike, moving forward and back and side-to-side to control the three-dimensional movement of the vehicle. She looked for the start button, noticing a green switch on the instrument panel.

"Okay," Riley said, quickly sizing up the controls. "But where's the *throttle* and *brake lever*? How do I make it speed up and slow down?"

Then she glanced toward the footwell, noticing two pedals.

"Maybe it's like the cars from back home," she said. "Could it really be that simple?"

She peered over her shoulder, noticing the cop and the guard grunting louder as they thrust their hips more rapidly against Ginger's body.

"It looks like I won't have much more time before their attention is diverted elsewhere," she said. "It's now or never. Let's see if this is as easy to fly as my hoverbike."

She flipped the green switch and when the engine growled to life, she tapped the right pedal, feeling the rotors above her beginning to turn. As the vehicle began to buffet on the helipad, the cop jerked his head around, pulling his cock out of Ginger's ass.

"What the fuck?" he said, noticing Riley sitting at the controls.

"Get in!" Riley yelled to Ginger, leaning over to push the passenger door open. "It's time to get the hell out of here!"

Ginger chomped her teeth down on the guard's hard-on and he hunched over, screaming in pain.

"Why you little–" the cop growled, reaching down to his pants bunched around his ankles to retrieve his service pistol.

As the helicopter began to rise slowly off the surface, he fired toward the crew compartment, shattering a hole in the glass. While Riley struggled to maintain control of the craft, it began spinning wildly over the pad. Then the cop swung around to the front of the compartment, aiming his laser pistol at Riley with two outstretched arms.

"The gig's up, Vega," he said. "Put that thing back down where it belongs or I'll give you another hole where you don't need it."

Riley steadied the helicopter, gazing at the cop through the glass canopy, realizing his laser pistol would pick her off before she had a chance to move out of range. But just as she was about to ease up on the joystick and lower the craft to the ground, she noticed the elevator door opening behind him. Suddenly, Talyn stepped out of the compartment, training her firearm at the cop.

"Put it down, Logan," she said, walking toward him slowly. "There's only two ways this can end."

The cop turned his head in Talyn's direction, then he swung his body around, trying to shoot her before she could react. Talyn fired her laser, striking him in the crotch, and he dropped his weapon, falling onto the tarmac.

"You shot me in my *dick!*" he screamed, thrusting his hands between his legs.

"Yeah, well, you won't be *needing* it where you'll be going for the next ten or twenty years. You'll just have to keep your fellow inmates amused using your *other* body parts."

Then Talyn looked up, noticing Riley watching her while hovering the helicopter a few feet off the ground. She raced around to the other side and opened the rear door, climbing in the back seat behind Ginger.

"Got room for one more?" she said.

"Took you long enough," Riley smiled, glancing at her girlfriend.

"Who's your new friend?" Talyn said, flaring her eyes at Ginger's voluptuous body.

"This is Ginger," Riley said. "She's the real hero in this scenario."

"Is there some reason why you're both *naked?*" Talyn said.

"I'll tell you all about it when we get back to the station," Riley smiled. "It's a bit of a long story."

14

———

"How did you know where to find me?" Riley said as they lifted off the heliport, watching a SWAT team swarming over the grounds of the villa.

"It wasn't very hard," Talyn said. "When I traced your signal and noticed it moving off the marked highways, I knew something was amiss. I tracked your route back to this location and when I saw the commotion on the helipad, our team decided to move in."

"What about Theta?" Riley said.

"He didn't go down the easy way," Talyn said, motioning to a body lying face down in the pool surrounded by a large red stain.

Riley nodded, then suddenly remembered there was one other piece of unfinished business.

"I overheard the helicopter pilot talking with him about some kind of prostitution ring involving underage girls. Apparently, they've been bypassing the normal immigration channels to kidnap orphans arriving from Earth–"

"I'll have the chief look into it as soon as we get back,"

Talyn nodded. "With Theta out of commission, we should be able to break the ring pretty quickly."

"Are you sure he can be trusted?" Riley said. "Theta said his contacts go pretty high up."

"I'll be looking into it personally," Talyn said. "Now that we have access to all of Theta's records and personal communications, it shouldn't be hard to expose the rest of the players."

"So that's the end of it?" Riley said, breathing a sigh of relief while she followed the tracking beacon back to the station.

"Until someone *else* decides to step into the void. There'll always be someone who's willing to risk his neck for a piece of the enormous profits to be made in the black market."

Some things never change, Riley thought to herself. *It seems that no matter where I go, greedy humans always have to mess things up.*

After they returned to the station and completed their debrief, the chief paid Riley her bounty, and the threesome retired to the lunchroom for some much-needed chow.

"So, what happens now?" Riley said, sitting across from Ginger while they stared at the orange jumpsuits the chief had given them to cover up their naked bodies.

"Well, for starters," Talyn said, glancing around the room while the other cops peered suspiciously at their prison uniforms. "I think we should get you into some more comfortable clothes."

"Yeah," Riley chuckled. "I'm not sure orange is my best color."

She peered at Ginger, watching the robot turning the food over on her lunch plate absent-mindedly.

"What about *you*, Ginger? What will you do now that you're a free woman?"

"I'm not sure," Ginger said. "I don't have anywhere to stay now that Theta's no longer looking after me. I'll just have to get by using my usual methods. Like Talyn said earlier, there's always a demand for pretty girls, even if they're synths."

"Fuck that," Riley said. "I promised that I'd take you away from all that when you helped me escape. It's time to stop acting like someone *else* is pulling the strings and take charge of your life like a normal person."

"But I wouldn't know where to start or where to go..." Ginger said.

"You're welcome to stay at my place for a while," Talyn smiled. "Any friend of Vega's is a friend of mine. I'm sure we can make space for one more girl in my cramped apartment."

"Really?" Ginger said, suddenly peering up at the two women with bright eyes. "You'd do that for me? Even though I'm just a–"

"Hey, we're all just a bundle of nerves and synapses when it gets down to it," Talyn said. "It shouldn't take long for you to develop your own identity like the rest of us, now that the cord has been cut."

"Now that you mention it," Riley said. "I *was* kind of looking forward to expanding her horizons now that she's free to pursue her own desires. How'd you like to try a *different* kind of threesome once we get home?"

"You mean the three of *us?*" Ginger said, raising her eyebrows.

"Why not?" Riley smiled. "There's no time like the present to begin your new education."

"Have you even experienced a real orgasm before?" Talyn said.

"You mean like a *man?*" Ginger said.

"Yes, except without all the messy bodily fluids."

"I'm programmed to simulate human pleasure," the robot nodded. "But I've never felt a climax in the same manner as my clients..."

"That's because you've been with the wrong kind of partners," Talyn said. "When you have sex with somebody who cares for you as a person, it becomes a whole different kind of experience."

"I like the sound of that," Ginger smiled. "When can we get started retraining my synapses?"

Riley suddenly put her spoon down, shuffling uncomfortably in her chair.

"I don't know about you guys," she said. "But I'm *already* beginning to emit some of those bodily fluids. Suddenly, I'm not hungry any longer..."

Reády *for more steamy chills and thrills? Read the next exciting volume in Riley's Time Travel Adventures, Ninja Assassin. Buy direct and save at victoriarusherotica. Or download from your favorite online bookstore here: retailer links.*

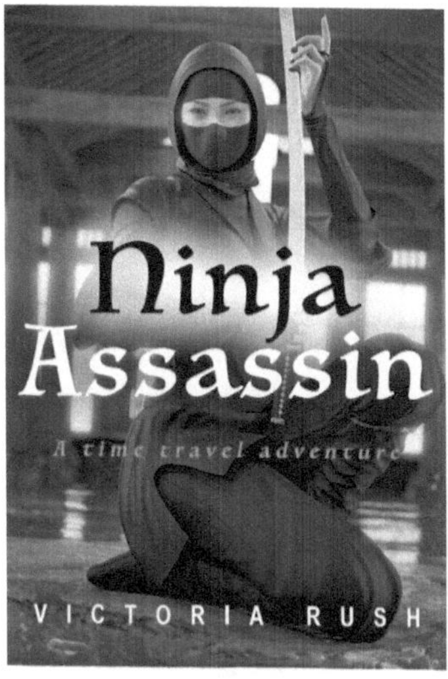

Some assassins have a conscience...

ALSO BY VICTORIA RUSH

Adult Fairytales:

The Enchanted Forest: An Erotic Fairytale

The Land of Giants: An Erotic Fairytale

The Dragon's Lair: An Erotic Fairytale

Witch's Brew: An Erotic Fairytale

The Mage's Spell: An Erotic Fairytale

The Mermaid Lagoon: An Erotic Fairytale

The Coven: An Erotic Fairytale

Rapunzel: An Erotic Fairytale

The Seven Dwarfs: An Erotic Fairytale

The Land of Mutants: An Erotic Fairytale

The Erotic Temple: A Sexy Fairytale (Coming Soon)

Erotica Themed Bundles:

Voyeur: Lesbian Erotica Bundle

Public Affairs: A Lesbian Anthology

Futa Fantasies: The Ladyboy Collection

Threesomes: The Lesbian Collection

Threesomes - Volume 2: The Lesbian Collection

First Time: A Lesbian Anthology

Hedonism: An Erotic Anthology

Switch Hitters: Bisexual Erotica

Taboo Erotica: The Lesbian Series

BDSM: The Lesbian Collection

Party Games: The Erotic Collection

Party Games 2: The Erotic Collection

All Girl 1: Lesbian Erotica Bundle

All Girl 2: Lesbian Erotica Bundle

All Girl 3: Lesbian Erotica Bundle

All Girl 4: Lesbian Erotica Bundle

Erotic Fairytale Bundles:

Clover's Fantasy Adventures: Books 1 - 5

Clover's Fantasy Adventures: Books 6 - 10

Erotic Fantasy:

Pirate's Bounty: A Time Travel Adventure

Wild West: A Time Travel Adventure

Private Riley: A Time Travel Adventure

Cleopatra's Secret: A Time Travel Adventure

Bounty Hunter 2125: A Time Travel Adventure

Ninja Assassin: A Time Travel Adventure

The 300: A Time Travel Adventure

Arabian Nights: An Erotic Fairytale (coming soon…)

Steamy Time Travel Bundles:

Riley's Time Travel Adventures: Books 1 - 5

Lesbian Erotica:

The Dinner Party: Lesbian Voyeur Erotica

The Darkroom: Bisexual Voyeur Erotica

Naked Yoga: Lesbian Transgender Erotica

Nude Cruise: Bisexual Voyeur Erotica

Rush Hour: Taboo Public Sex

The Girl Next Door: First Time Lesbian Erotic Romance

Girls' Camp: Lesbian Group Sex

Wet Dream: Ladyboy Fantasy Erotica

The Convent: Taboo Sex with a Nun

Sex Robot: A Dream Sex Machine

The Personal Trainer: Getting Pumped at the Gym

The Dominatrix: BDSM Lesbian Domination

Webcam Chat: Lesbian Online Sex

Paint Me: A Kinky Bodypainting Workshop

The Toy Party: Girls Sharing Sex Toys

The Costume Party: Strapping One On

Swedish Sauna: Lesbian Group Sex

The Therapist: Taboo Lesbian Erotica

Elevator Shaft: Bisexual Threesomes Erotica

Ladyboy: Lesbian Transgender Erotica

Peep Show: Lesbian Voyeur Erotica

The Dare: Public Sex Erotica

Maid Service: Lesbian Threesomes Erotica

The Hitchhiker: First Time Lesbian Erotica

The Housesitter: Spycam Lesbian Erotica

The Spa: Lesbian Group Orgy

Parlor Games: Blindfold Sex Party

The Exchange Student: First Time Lesbian Erotica

The Hostel: Bisexual Group Erotica

The Harem: Lesbian Erotic Romance

The Orient Express: Lesbian Voyeur Erotica

The First Lady: A Forbidden Lesbian Erotic Romance

The Slave: Lesbian BDSM Erotica

The Masseuse: Lesbian Sensuous Erotica

Too Close for Comfort: Lesbian Forbidden Erotica

Naked Twister: A Wild Party Game

Lexi: The Sex App (Lesbian Fantasy Erotica)

Call Girl: Lesbian Bisexual Threesomes Erotica

Circle Jill: Lesbian Masturbation Workshop

The Viewing Room: Masturbation Voyeur Erotica

Spin the Bottle: A Kinky Party Game

The Hair Salon: Lesbian Voyeur Erotica

Tribadism 1: Girls Only Sex Workshop

Tribadism 2: The Art of Scissoring

Tribadism 3: Threeway Hookups

The Kiss: A Game of Oral Sex

Pledge Week: Sorority Sisters

Carny Games 1: A Wild Sex Party

Carny Games 2: A Kinky Sex Party

Carny Games 3: An Erotic Sex Party

Dreamscape: An Artificial Reality Game

Glory Hole: Guess Who's On the Other Side

Joy Ride: A Late Night Erotic Bus Trip

The Blind Girl: An Erotic Romance(Coming Soon)

Lesbian Erotica Bundles:

Jade's Erotic Adventures: Books 1 - 5

Jade's Erotic Adventures: Books 6 - 10

Jade's Erotic Adventures: Books 11 - 15

Jade's Erotic Adventures: Books 16 - 20

Jade's Erotic Adventures: Books 21 - 25

Jade's Erotic Adventures: Books 26 - 30

Jade's Erotic Adventures: Books 31 - 35

Jade's Erotic Adventures: Books 36 - 40

Jade's Erotic Adventures: Books 41 - 45

Jade's Erotic Adventures: Books 46 - 50

Fifty Shades of Jade: Superbundle

Standalone Stories:

The Polynesian Girl: A Lesbian EroticRomance